united p.c.

Printed in the European Union,

www.united-pc.eu

JAMES M DYET'S

YOU CAN'T BUY LOVE

=====

WHITE LIES

=====

WHY ME

JAMES M DYET'S

YOU CAN'T BUY LOVE

YOU CAN'T BUY LOVE

WHEN YOU LOOK FOR LOVE IT HIDES.

A QUITE TRIP TO THE COAST BROUGHT LOVE BUT ALONG WITH IT CAME CONSPIRACY AND MURDER.

YOU CAN'T BUY LOVE

YOU CAN'T BUY LOVE

It only seems like yesterday that I was in my nice cosy flat, it was modest; nevertheless I loved it, now here I sit in a big expensive house in the country. How did I get here? Well, I will tell you.

It all started last November when I decided I would have a day at the coast, I thought I would head for Bexhill as it was full of nice shops and cafes, I had a strange pleasant nostalgic feeling about the place so I got my wallet, keys etc and went to my old but comfortable Sierra car; there was mist in the air and it was damp and cold, I went back in put my warm jacket on and set off feeling nice and relaxed.

By the time I reached the outskirts of Bexhill the mist had disappeared and the sun had started to come out, I noticed a well dressed man in a suit sitting on the kerbside with his elbows on his knees and head in his hands.

As it was about three miles from anywhere I pulled over and asked if his car had broken down, not that I could see one, I asked if he would like a lift into Bexhill, the man just stayed in the same motionless position, I got out of the car and when I got closer I could see his suit was wet from the early morning mist; Is he dead? I asked myself.
"Are you ok; you're wet from the dew?"
There was no reply, he lifted his head and slowly shook it from side to side.
"What's up, are you hurt?"
He shook his head but never answered me, as he raised his head higher I could see his face was pale and his sad eyes stared not at me but straight ahead.
"My name is Tom, come on let's get a cuppa and something to eat; my shout."
To my surprise he stood up but rather unsteadily, so I helped him to my car. He was well built and must have been around 6'4" tall, as I am only 5'10" he seemed to tower above me and felt like a brick wall leaning on me.

As we drove off he stared straight ahead with a desperate look in his eyes;

all the way to Bexhill he said nothing, he was distant and stared at the floor.

I pulled over outside a little cafe in Bexhill that I had been to many times before; a dear old woman with a heart of gold ran it.
“Hello Tom, Black coffee with One and a half sugars?”
She chuckled as she always thought it funny. I turned to the man beside me.
“Tea, Milk and two sugars?” I asked.
Without looking up he nodded.
“How about I buy you a good English breakfast?”
For the first time he looked at me and gave a small smile, I guided him to a small table by the heater which he moved close to. We sat quietly waiting then the old woman I knew as Sophie returned with our drinks, her silver hair seemed to sparkle like her eyes and her smile was comforting.
“Thank you Sophie.” I said as we sipped our tea. I asked him if he was in this state because his mother-in-law was coming to stay, he grinned.
“It’s worse than that.”
He replied in a worried voice.

"What could be worse than that?"
He didn't reply but carried on hugging his cup and sipping his tea. I called out to Sophie.
"I think I will have something to eat Sophie, please."
"Beans on toast with a free range egg on top?" Sophie said jokingly.
"How did you know?" I asked.
"Woman's intuition I suppose."
She said grinning and disappeared into the kitchen. The man beside me said.
"Eat here a lot?"
I nodded and smiled.
"I don't get to Bexhill that often but I always come here to eat when I do."
He looked around the café suspiciously; just an old couple were in the cafe apart from us.
"It looks like your breakfast is on its way." I said cheerfully hoping to put him at ease, Sophie put the plate down in front of him, a look of amazement appeared on his face and his eyes opened wide, he turned to look at her.
"Thank you, thank you very much; Tom's paying."
"Thanks, Tom." she replied as she patted me on my back.

The man ate slowly to begin with and then he got stuck in as mine arrived. Afterwards we thanked Sophie and left.

The sun was out and it was starting to feel warm so I looked at him and said.
"Fancy a stroll on the beach to walk the breakfast off?"
He nodded in agreement.

The man never spoke as we walked but remained deep in thought. I stopped, picked up a pebble and skimmed it across the fairly calm sea.
"That was a good throw." I said.
"Three bounces."
He looked at me with a puzzled expression on his face.
"Bet you can't beat that."
I continued, trying to cheer him up.
He stared down at the beach and then he stooped down and with a grunt threw a pebble across the waves.
(Plop) it went straight into the water.
"Oh, hard luck" I said and started to laugh. A big grin spread across his face and he threw one after another. When he threw his tenth pebble he got six

bounces, I looked at him.
His eyes gleamed with excitement.
“How did I do?” He asked.
I looked at him with a sad expression on my face.
“That’s it. I’m not playing any more.”
I replied and started to laugh.
“I’ve never got more than four that was brilliant, well Burt where shall we go to now?”
“How did you know my name?”
He said, surprised.
“So your name is Burt?”
“No it’s Sidney, everyone calls me Sid.”
“Well Sid let us have a walk round the town.”

I like the charity shops in Bexhill and there was one nearby, Sid just stood outside looking awkward.
“Come on in you old snob.” I said.
He muttered that he wasn’t a snob and followed me inside; he went all over the shop looking at everything with an amazed look on his face at the reasonable prices, I noticed he picked up a pocket watch and stared at it.
“That’s nice.” I said.
He quickly put it back and made for the

door. We left but as we started to walk away I said.
"I think I will buy that wallet as mine is a bit worn."

After I came back out we returned to Sophie's cafe for another cuppa. Sid looked extremely worried as he stared into his teacup.
"Don't let it get cold."
I said without looking up.
"I can't pay you back; I have no money, not even a watch to my name."
"I don't want your money and as for not having a watch, that's not true."
I placed the watch Sid had seen in the charity shop on the table in front of him.
"Why?" he asked.
"I wanted to buy the wallet but as you looked more excited about the pocket watch than I was about the wallet, it made more sense to buy the watch."
Sid picked up the watch, flipped open the lid and after winding it up and putting it to the correct time he sat looking at it with a satisfied look on his face. The look on his face turned to despair.
"I can't face her, I've lost everything and

it's all gone, even our home."
"That's a neat trick, how did you work that?"
I waited not knowing what else to say. Sid clenched his fist and brought it up in front of his face then angrily said.
"They cheated; it was all a con, what could I do against three big men?"
"What are you talking about how could they get your house?"
"It was supposed to be a friendly game of cards; I thought they were joking about the amount, by the time I realised what was happening I owed them fifty grand; they got nasty when I reminded them it was just a friendly game and they kept dealing hands until they had my car, its worth 27 grand and the house is worth £1.5 million; I had to sign the paper or they would have killed me; the house belongs to my wife she is the one with money not me, they even took my wallet, my credit cards and made me tell them the pin codes for the cards."
"Do you remember what time they dropped you off at the side of the road?"
"About four am, then they threatened to kill me and my wife if I went to the

police."
"Well Sid I think the first thing to do is warn your wife, do you live far from here?"
"I live about ten miles away but I can't face her."
"As you don't have a car I could take you home and explain to your wife what has happened while you wait in the car, if that would help?"
"Thanks Tom I don't know what I would have done if you hadn't come along."

We made our way back to my car and Sid gave me the directions, then he began wringing his hands together and shaking. We had gone about four miles and by this time Sid was nearly in tears and becoming increasingly distressed, so I pulled over to a pub.
"It's ten o'clock and its open, I think you need a drink."
Sid downed two double whiskies and I had a black coffee then we set off again. Within five minutes he was fast asleep. How was I going to break the news to his wife!

We arrived at the beginning of Sid's drive and he was still fast asleep.

As the large mansion came into view I looked at Sid and wondered how someone like him could live in a place like this, I thought its true you can't tell just by looking at someone.
I parked the car about ten feet to the left of the front door so as not to alarm Sid's wife, I closed the car door quietly behind me so as not to wake Sid, then climbed the steps to the front door and banged the big brass owl door knocker. As I did so my mind went blank, panic I suppose but I was even more anxious when the door opened and a slim very attractive woman with long shining chestnut hair stood in front of me.
"Can I help you?"
"My name is Tom Logan and I have some bad news about your husband Sidney."
She invited me into the lobby.
"The police have already told me."
"Told you what?"
I asked feeling slightly confused.
"Apparently he never stood a chance; an articulated lorry went out of control and took my husband's car with it as it went off the high bridge and exploded."
"Are they sure it was Sid's car?"

"They only knew it was Sid's car because they found the rear number plate, the car was burnt out, why are you asking me if you already know about Sid?"
Just then Sid staggered through the open front door.
Sid's wife stood and stared at Sid, her mouth open and her face went a ghostly white.
"Who was in the car, who, tell me?" She shouted hysterically. Before Sid could say anything, I said.
"Sid was mugged by three men who stole everything including his car; he is still in a state of shock."
Sid looked at me with a look of triumph on his face before turning to his wife.
"What do you mean who was in the car, what car?" Sid asked.
"The police came here this morning about five thirty and said you had been killed in a road accident."
"Everything in the car was destroyed by fire." I added looking at Sid.
"Everything!" said Sid, looking relieved.
"When did you get mugged, was it before or after your game? You think I'm stupid! I know you were gambling

again." Sid's wife's said in anger.
"Only a friendly game with some men, they approached me as I left the meeting." Replied Sid.
"Did you know these men? Only it seems funny they should approach a complete stranger." She said.
"Never seen them before and they were nothing to do with our firm."

Sid started towards the front room muttering he needed another drink, before he got to the door his wife grabbed his arm and pulled him towards the kitchen and said.
"Let's go to the kitchen and we can all have something to eat and drink."
As they disappeared through the kitchen door, I rushed over to the front room to see why Sid's wife was reluctant to let Sid into the front room.
"Tom hurry up we are in the kitchen." Sid shouted.
"I'm just coming." I shouted back as my eyes quickly scanned the front room. So that's what she didn't want Sid to see, I thought to myself and then I rushed off in the direction of the kitchen.
"Shall we all have cheese and onion

sandwiches?" Sid's wife asked.
"That sounds good to me." I replied.
"Sid never told me your name."
"It's Ann, how do you like your tea?"
"No milk, one and a half sugars, thanks." I replied.

As we all started our lunch I looked at Sid and Ann and tried to figure out what was going on, by the time we had finished I had a couple of theories.
Ann asked if anyone wanted another cup of tea and both Sid and I nodded. Ann got up to top up the kettle and looked at the clock again, she seemed to do this every five minutes.
The telephone in the other room started to ring, Ann swung round slopping water all over the floor as she slammed the kettle down on the worktop, she seemed to panic in an effort to beat Sid to the phone, she slipped on the wet floor and fell backwards hitting her head on the floor.
Sid and I rushed to her aid and Sid tried talking to Ann but she was out cold. By this time the phone had stopped ringing.
"Do you think we should phone a

doctor, Sid? Be best because she might have concussion."
"That's a good idea Tom, I will do that now."

He headed for the front room where the telephone was and I followed him to see what his reaction would be when he got there. He stared at the five suitcases which confronted him.
"What's up, Sid?" Pretending not to notice the suitcases.
"Where was she going and who do those two cases belong to?"
"Ann was probably going to surprise you." I answered as Sid went straight to one of the cases and opened it.
"Look! She hasn't worn stuff like this since our honeymoon 24 years ago."
I looked over his shoulder and saw it was full of silky nightgowns and underwear.
"You lucky old thing, it looks like your going on a second honeymoon."
Sid began to stare at the two suitcases he didn't recognise. He grabbed one and opened it, tipped the contents on the floor saying as he did so.
"These are not mine, what the hell is

going on?"
Just then the phone bleeped twice.
"The caller must have left a message."
Sid said as he crossed to the phone and pressed the loud speaker on the playback. A man's voice said.
"Hello darling guess you are getting ready? I hope to be with you about 1 pm; that will give us enough time to get to the airport, I can't wait; I still haven't heard from my three mates since they conned your old man out of everything; I told them to leave him his car and then got another mate to fix it, when it hits 65mph the electrics would fry and the only place your old man would do over that speed would be on a motorway; as you haven't given me the signal that he is home he must be out of the way, See you later darling."
Sid stood very still and I could see that his eyes were starting to fill with tears and by the look on his face he was devastated.
I stood there unable to think of anything to say, just waiting to see what Sid was going to do next but he just stood still staring at the phone with tears running down his cheeks.

Plucking up courage I put my hand on his shoulder and told him to sit down while I telephoned for an ambulance for Ann. Sid covered his face with his hands as I led him to an armchair where he just sat staring at the floor.

Before phoning I went back to the kitchen to see if Ann had come to but she was still out cold, I looked at her lying on the floor thinking how attractive she looks, how will Sid get over losing her? Whatever happens she will probably end up in prison for planning to kill him.

I went back to the front room, Sid was slumped in the armchair and appeared to be asleep so I phoned for an ambulance and then phoned the police. I told them to arrive before I pm and asked them to put their car round the back of the house, so the lover wouldn't see it when he arrived. I asked Sid if he would like a glass of whiskey but he didn't respond so I went to the kitchen took my jacket off and placed it under Ann's head, I then took a blanket off the clean pile of washing and put it over Ann to keep her warm.

It seemed like hours before the ambulance arrived, in reality it was more like 25 minutes.

I opened the front door for the paramedics and explained to them what had happened. After examining Ann they put her on a stretcher and took her to the ambulance; one returned and examined Sid.
“We had better get him to hospital as he appears to be in shock.”
The paramedic seemed more concerned about Sid than Ann.
“Best if you keep them apart at the hospital until the police get there.”
I said feeling concerned about Sid’s reactions.
"Why are the police involved?”
The paramedic asked.
“He never touched her if that’s what you’re thinking, it’s a bit complicated.”
The paramedic nodded, fetched his partner and helped Sid to the ambulance before speeding off.

I returned to the kitchen, picked up my jacket and put it back on, then neatly folded the blanket before putting it back on the pile of clean washing.

After making myself a cup of tea I went back to the front room and recorded the message on my mobile just in case it was erased.

I sat by the window to wait for the police and glancing across the room I noticed a small bag on top of one of the cases, I decided to take a quick look at the contents, there were two flight tickets one in the name of Ann Gale and the other for someone called Adrian Brown; I put both tickets in my inside pocket before zipping the bag back up and putting it back.

A car came slowly down the drive and disappeared round the back of the house so I quickly went to the back door, as I opened it a man in a smart suit emerged.
I looked at the clock thinking it might be one o'clock but it was only 12.15 pm.
"I hope he's not early." I said.
"Who are you?"
"I think I should be asking you that don't you?" I replied.
"I am off duty but I heard a call over the radio saying the police were needed to attend an accident at this property, as I

was nearby I thought I would call."
I asked to see his badge; he flashed it in front of me and then hastily returned it to his pocket. I saw his picture and the words police inspector on the card, I told him that the lady had slipped over and knocked her self-out and she has been taken by ambulance to hospital, the reason the police were called was because of a message that had been left on the answering machine.
"Who listened to the message?"
He asked, sounding annoyed.
"Her husband." I replied cautiously.
"Who else has heard the message and where is her husband?"
"Only her husband has heard it and he is also in hospital."
"So who are you and what are you doing here?"
"I am a good friend of her husband's and I've been left in charge of the house until they get back, my name is Tom Logan."
"Where's the phone?" he demanded.
After I showed him where the phone was he unplugged it and asked me what the message said.
"I've already told you, the only one that

listened to it was her husband."
He looked angry about something and stormed back to his car with the phone.

I felt really hungry so I made some toast and started frying a couple of eggs when there was a knock on the back door. A police car was parked outside and a plain clothed man stood on the step, he apologised for not getting here earlier and said it was only 12.40 pm, he asked if the man he had come to arrest had been round yet.
"No" I replied. "But you're not late as your inspector has just left."
He looked puzzled.
"Come in, would you like a cuppa? Hang on my eggs are burning!"
I removed the eggs from the hob and made the policeman a cup of tea; while I was eating I saw the policeman reading a letter that Ann had left on the kitchen table.
"That's rude." I said and put the letter on the welsh dresser. He apologised and said. "Sorry force of habit."
He was confused about this inspector who had just left and asked me for his name.

"He didn't give me one, he just showed me his card, I only saw his photo and the words 'police inspector; He took the phone with the message on it but I took his car registration."
I handed it to the policeman who made a telephone call. He then told me that the car had been reported stolen that morning and asked me for a description of the man. I told him that the man was about 5'10" tall with light brown hair, he had a moustache, thin face and a small scar on his chin, probably from a safety razor; he wore a grey suit and black shoes. I told the officer that I hadn't noticed any wristwatch or rings but that I thought he may be on his way to the hospital to see her husband."
I looked at the officer.
"I wouldn't trust him."
I said in a low voice and then added.
"Do you know him? Wouldn't be someone called Adrian would it?"
"Don't know of anyone by that name on the force."
"Do you know an Inspector Brown on the force?"
"No; No Inspector Brown on the force, it's now gone 1 pm and no one has

turned up yet."
We sat drinking our tea and looking at the clock, it seemed to tick louder as the minutes passed.
"I don't think he's coming, Ann and this man were going to catch a flight at 3 pm, it's now 2.15 pm and there's no way they could make it to the airport and catch the flight now."
"How do you know that?"
The officer asked; I took the tickets out of my pocket and put them down on the table in front of him and after looking at them he said.
"That's where you got the names from, anything else you haven't told me about?"
"I would like to know who I am talking to first; can I see your ID?"
The man nodded and produced his details. His name was Inspector Alan Abbott, so then I continued.
"The other man that came was concerned about who had heard the message on the phone, I told him only Ann's husband Sid; He then rushed off but he did say he heard about the lady's accident on his radio in his car and he was off duty."

Inspector Abbott said that without the message they had no case, he telephoned the hospital in case the man had turned up there. He then phoned for a patrol car to go to the hospital and then he left.

I phoned the hospital to see how Sid and Ann were and after telling them I was Sid's brother, they told me that Sid refused to talk to anyone and that Ann had regained consciousness; they told me Ann seemed okay but they were keeping her in overnight to be on the safe side and Ann had ordered a taxi for 9am tomorrow morning to take her home. They informed me that until Sid ate or drank anything he would be kept in and possibly put on a drip.

I found a blanket in the airing cupboard and after making up a bed on the settee I settled down to watch television until about 10 pm. Feeling very tired I closed my eyes and drifted off to sleep.

The alarm on my mobile phone woke me at 7 am. I rose and after putting the blanket away I made myself some tea and toast, afterwards I

returned to the front room to tidy up the suitcases Sid had opened just so Ann wouldn't know what Sid had seen. I repacked the man's clothing and did Ann's suitcase back up, then I decided to check what was in the other suitcases. One of the unknown cases contained women's clothes.
The two cases Sid recognised had women's clothes in one and it looked as if the other suitcase contained Sid's clothes. I picked up the bag in which I had discovered the tickets and found an envelope that hadn't been sealed. There were two more air tickets – one for Sid Gale and one for May Brown, so I went back to the kitchen and picked up the other two tickets from the table. One was in the name of Adrian Brown and the other was in the name of Ann Gale. The tickets must have got muddled up. Poor Sid is thinking all the wrong things, what on earth was that phone message about, nothing made sense? I put everything back where I found it then made a coffee and waited for Ann to arrive.

It was about 9.40am when the taxi arrived. I opened the front door and noticed Ann looked pale and sad.
I asked if she was okay and offered to make her a cup of tea, she nodded and so I followed her to the kitchen where she sat down. After putting the kettle on I looked at Ann and asked how Sid was doing.
"What's going on Tom? Why has Sid gone like that? Everything was going great so what happened after I was knocked out? Please tell me."
I told Ann everything that had happened and let her listen to the message on my phone. She just sat there, a wild look on her face which changed to sadness as she looked at me and said.
"It's that creep, it must be him, what is he playing at?"
"Who is this man? Not Adrian Brown!" I exclaimed.
"No, Adrian and May have bought a villa in Madrid and they invited Sid and myself to stay for a month, it would be just like a second honeymoon for us and now it's all spoiled."
"When are you supposed to go to Madrid, Ann?"

"Another four days and we would have been on our way Tom."
"Who is this man that left the message Ann and why would he want to kill Sid?"
"His name is Simon Patterson, he was in the police force but was dismissed, he was caught selling drugs and trying to force women to go with him including me."
"But why would he pick on you."
"He thinks it was me that got him the sack, he must have my phone tapped because he knew about the air tickets, even Sid never knew about them."
"This Patterson must have set Sid up but didn't reckon on his mates getting greedy and keeping the car, he alone is responsible for the three dead men and he knows Sid is still alive, I had better phone the police on my mobile, I can't risk using your phone."

After speaking to inspector Abbott I told Ann we had better go to the hospital and put Sid straight about the suitcases and the message on the phone.
"Thank you Tom you have been wonderful."

She gave me a big hug and a kiss on the cheek which caught me off guard making me feel embarrassed.
“Are you okay Tom you look flushed?”
“I’m fine, I Just had a shock to the system, I will bring my car round to the back so you can get in unseen just in case Patterson is watching the house.”

I pulled up just as Ann was locking the back door, looking excited as she started towards the car.
“I will lie on the back seat until we get on our way.” Ann said excitedly.

We had driven about a mile when Ann asked if she could get in the front with me, I pulled over and Ann climbed into the front passenger seat before we carried on our way. She looked just like a child who was going to the coast for the first time.
“Sid’s a very lucky man, everything in his life seems perfect and it’s a shame this has happened to spoil things.”
She just looked at me and smiled, a sad expression appeared on her face and she went quiet until we reached the hospital.

The receptionist told us where to find Sid but as we approached the ward Sid was coming down the corridor arm in arm with a rather dishy woman. The woman was attractive and wearing a tight Minnie skirt and looked like she should be standing on a street corner.
"What's going on, Sid? We have come to pick you up and take you home."
Ann said sounding very upset.
"It's been a big mix-up Sid, the message on the phone was made up by someone to break you and Ann up and none of it was true, except the crash."
I explained hoping to put him straight but he turned to Ann and said.
"We are finished Ann, I am going to make a new life with Tracey."
He held Tracey's arm firmly and walked past, Ann burst into tears and sank to the floor leaving me completely confused about everything.
"Come on let's get you home, perhaps once I talk to Sid he will come back."
I felt helpless as I helped her up and then she said.
"All he wants me for is my money, it's not the first time he has cleared off with her."

"He can't be serious about leaving you."
"Thought I could win him back with a second honeymoon."
"Don't you think he will come back this time Ann."
"He always comes back when he runs out of money."

When we got back to Ann's house a police car was waiting in the drive; Ann invited inspector Abbott in and he told her that Simon Patterson could not have been involved, mainly because he has been in prison for the last ten months and still had two years to serve for fraud.
The Inspector explained that they had picked up the man who had called and taken the telephone, he made a full statement after they had charged him with murder.
Inspector Abbott had contacted the hospital, they told him that Sid had already left and he had come to Ann's to arrest him.
Ann looked as shocked as I felt. "Why." she exclaimed.
"Your husband set the whole thing up, If Mr Logan had not picked him up you

would be in the morgue now. All he wanted was your money, not you."
Ann slumped into a chair, a look of disbelief on her face.
Ann explained to Inspector Abbott that Tracey Kemp lived somewhere in Eastbourne and worked at one of the banks.
"That's all I know about her, apart from the fact she can't keep her hands off other women's husbands."
Inspector Abbott said he would be in touch and left.

I looked at Ann and said I was sorry that all this had happened to her and that I hoped things would work out okay. I felt it was time for me to go home but as I turned to leave Ann grabbed my arm and swung me round, she looked into my eyes briefly before giving me a hug.
She asked if I could stay for the evening and she would cook dinner, then suggested we watch a film afterwards, she was scared and did not want to be on her own tonight.
As all I had to look forward to was an empty flat and only bread, cheese and

beans in the cupboard, a good cooked dinner sounded good.
"That would be great."
I said and asked if I could help with the preparation.
"That would be nice, normally I have to do it all on my own; Tom what would you like to eat?"
"I don't eat meat or fish, Sorry."
"Nor do I, fancy a baked potato with cheese and vegetables?"
"Say no more, give me the spuds and I will get them on."
"Would you like some wine with your dinner?" she offered.
"Can't, I've got to drive home; I don't want to lose my licence."
"There's a spare bed here, in fact there are four spare bedrooms; please stay the night and I will do you a nice big breakfast in the morning."
"Okay Ann, sounds good."
"I will make up the bed in the bedroom next to mine in case there is any trouble and then you won't be so far away; thank you for everything Tom."

We dished up dinner at the kitchen table, poured the wine and sat

down to enjoy the meal.
Ann looked happy and kept smiling at me, making me blush, we never spoke until we had finished eating, after which we took our glasses of wine and the bottle to the TV room. I sat on the settee while Ann fetched a DVD.
"What are we going to watch, Ann?"
"I like to watch all types of films what about a comedy Tom?"
"That sounds good to me."
Ann sat at the other end of the settee and gave me a big smile, she picked up her glass and sat back to watch the film. She laughed so much the tears started to roll down her cheeks and then she got up and refilled our wine glasses. She sat down next to me still laughing and put her arm round across my shoulders; she gave me a hug and kissed me on the cheek.
I felt very uneasy and felt a bit panicky.
"Thanks Tom thanks for everything."
We sat back and finished watching the film and the wine relaxed me a bit.
Ann fetched another bottle of wine and filled our glasses.
"Best evening I have had for months, it's been wonderful."

She said excitedly.
"Don't you and Sid spend evenings together? He seemed a nice bloke when we were in Bexhill, I'm a bit confused."
"We are like strangers, I love Sid but we have nothing in common, we spend evenings apart and haven't been intimate for months; what's wrong with me Tom, why am I not attractive?"
"Ann, you are very attractive and good company I can't understand why Sid could ever want anyone else; you have nothing to blame yourself for."
"Are you serious Tom? Sid has never made me feel like that."
"Have you had an affair or done something to hurt Sid Ann? You are a very desirable woman and it doesn't make sense to me."
"Sid was in love with Tracey before we met, she dumped Sid when she fell for a rich playboy and went abroad with him, I didn't know Sid was still in love with someone else until after we had married."
"How did you know he was unfaithful?"
"He got drunk one night and told me we were never that close; after that he

started staying out some nights, so I got a private investigator to check on him."
"That seems a bit drastic Ann."
"I had to, my life was falling apart."
"What was the outcome?"
"Cost me quite a bit of money Tom but Tracey had been dumped for someone else and she had come back to live in Britain, Shame she chose Eastbourne."
"How did she get back in with Sid?"
"It wasn't long before she phoned Sid up where he worked and got him under her spell again, he is still madly in love with her."
"Did you tell Sid what you had found out and how?"
"No, I hoped if I spoiled Sid and bought him nice things he would choose me and forget her, what a fool I was to think I could buy his love."
"Are you still in love with him Ann?"
"I thought I was but after spending the evening with you Tom I found out what true love is; I have fallen deeply in love with someone else Tom."
I looked at Ann and my eyes felt watery.
"I don't know what to say except good luck, I hope you get your wish."
"Tom, you look very upset, why? I

thought you liked being with me."
"I love being with you, I guess I got carried away and thought wrong, I won't see you again; god bless you, I wish you all the best. I will leave for home first thing in the morning and thank you for a wonderful evening."
I got up and so did Ann, I gave her a hug and was about to give her a peck on the cheek when she grabbed me and gave me a long loving kiss on the lips; I stood there in disbelief.
"It's you I have fallen in love with Tom, no one has ever shown me such respect or caring, I don't really know what it is but I just want to be near you all the time, I feel such a fool."
I just stood there feeling numb from head to toe and unable to speak.
"Please don't leave, if you don't love me then perhaps we can still be friends?"
"Ann, not in my wildest dreams could I ever have imagined being with someone as beautiful and wonderful as you, I have never felt like this in my life."
Ann stared at me for a second or two before starting to cry. We both cuddled up on the settee and said nothing for a while; I gave her a squeeze and told her

perhaps we should get a good night's sleep. I suggested perhaps she should sleep on it and see if she still felt the same in the morning; I would respect her wishes whatever she decided.

Ann turned off the lights and we made our way up the carved wooden staircase. Still cuddling each other Ann took me by the hand and led me to a panelled door. In fact all the doors on the landing were old oak with deep panels. When Ann opened the door and put on the light I was amazed to see a big four-poster bed made of heavy old oak and hung with ruby red silk drapes. There were matching sheets a thick deep pile gold carpet, on the cream walls hung pictures of 'Old England' in gold frames and a beautiful chandelier hung from the ceiling.
"What do you think Tom, do you like it? I really love it"
"Breathe taking, really lovely."
I answered.
"Where's my room?"
"Don't you want to sleep with me Tom?"
"Like nothing better Ann but let's wait until you are sure first, best sleep on it

and be positive it's me you want."
Ann looked a bit put out and took me to the adjoining room and opened the door. Moonlight cut a wide path across the room from the window to the door making the rest of the room appear very dark. Ann turned on the light; it could have been called the blue room. Light blue walls, dark blue doors and a mid blue carpet. The bedding was blue and gold silk trim; there was the added luxury of an en suite bathroom.
"Thank you Ann, I will see you in the morning."
Ann gave me a hug and a kiss on the cheek and said.
"Pleasant dreams, you know where I am if you change your mind."

She left the room and closed the door behind her. I felt awkward letting Ann down but thought it was in her best interests, so I got ready for bed.
Ann had left a new pair of silk pyjamas on the bed, probably a pair she had bought for Sid for their holiday.
I switched on the bedside light before turning off the main light and climbed into the double bed before turning off

the bedside light again. The only light in the room was from the moon shining across the carpet. I snuggled down and soon fell asleep.

I don't remember anything more until I was woken by an extremely cold draught across my face. When I opened my eyes I could see that it was 4 am from the bedside clock's illuminated display. I noticed that the window was half-open, the moon still lit up the bedroom door which I noticed was now open. I caught a glimpse of a figure turning into the landing in the direction of Ann's room. Silently I slipped out of bed and my feet sank into the deep piled carpet. Looking out of the half-opened window I spotted a telescopic ladder leaning against the wall. Thanks to the carpet I made no sound as I made my way to Ann's room. The door was open and the room was in darkness except for the moonlight coming through the window, it lit up a figure standing at the end of Ann's bed. The intruder raised their right arm and I could see there was something in their hand which was pointed at the mound

of Ann's body under the quilt. Four shots rang out before I could reach the intruder. I shouted "No" and as the intruder turned their head I smashed my fist into the right-hand side of their face. The intruder hit their head on the corner post as they fell, I rushed to light switch and switched it on.
As I reached the bottom of the bed I could see where the bullets had pierced the quilt, four across her back. There was no way Ann could still be alive. All I could see was her shining hair showing above the quilt, I couldn't bear to pull the quilt back and as I turned and looked at the murderer I felt very evil towards the figure lying face down in the carpet.
The gun was lying by their side and I noticed that the murderer was wearing disposable gloves. As I turned the body over I could hardly believe my eyes, it was Inspector Abbott.
I removed his gloves, put them on and opened the window; I put his fingerprints all over the gun and placed the gun in Inspector Abbott's right hand, then fired the last two shots through the open window so that Forensics would

be able to prove that Abbott had fired the gun. I let go of his hand which slipped lifelessly to the carpet, the gun still in his hand and after shutting the window I took a rope tie holding back the curtain and bent down to tie his hands.

Before I could get his hands together a man's voice said loudly. "You just can't keep your nose out of it, can you?"
I looked towards the door; there stood the man who had taken the telephone. "What's this all about, why did Abbott kill Ann and what are you doing here?"
"I will have to kill you too, if you want to know Abbott thought he had no living relative that was until he did some research and found he did have one, the late Ann over there. As Ann was rich and was married Abbott decided Ann and Sid would both have to die, then Abbott would get the lot."
"What about the men who died in the car?" I asked.
"They were in on it, to make Sid think he had lost everything, I rigged Sid's car so they would be killed and I told them

to take it as they had served their purpose. Abbott was to pick Sid up, take him home and tell him Ann was having affairs with two men, he hoped Sid would kill her and to make sure I left that message. Ann had made plans to be out until the afternoon but must have decided to stay home."

"How do you know Ann had made plans?"

"I tapped the phone, things went wrong when you picked Sid up; Still Ann is dead and we know where Sid is. When you are out of the way we will kill Sid and make it look like he found you two in bed, killed both of you and then he killed himself. Then it is just Abbott and me with all that money."

"Wrong, it's just me."

Abbott had come to and had picked up the gun. He was pointing it at the man in the doorway but when he pulled the trigger it just clicked. He didn't know I had fired the last two bullets through the window while he was out cold.

"Stupid!" the man in the doorway shouted at Abbott then shot him. Abbott fell backwards and slumped against the wall; the man in the

doorway raised his gun and pointed it at me. I quickly grabbed a thick silver tray off Ann's dressing table and held it in front of my chest, but just as I was going to rush towards him there was a loud clang, his eyes stared up at the ceiling and he dropped to his knees. My eyes followed him down, I looked at the tray but there was no dent in it.
A voice said.
"I told you it was that creep."
There in the doorway stood Ann in a ruby red satin nightdress, both hands holding the handle of a badly dented bed warming pan.
Her face was as red as her nightdress.
"Thank goodness you are okay; I thought I had lost you!"
I rushed over to Ann who dropped the warming pan.
Wrapping my arms around her I gave her a long and loving kiss.
"Wow, Tom, you do care, I could do with some more of them."
"Who is that in your bed and where did you come from?"
"I couldn't sleep so I crept into your bed hoping to change your mind but you were in a deep sleep, so I let Mildred

have my bed and fell asleep next to you."
"I'm sorry Ann but Mildred is dead."
"I heard everything Tom."
Ann took my hand and led me to her bed and pulled back the quilt.
"It's a full sized model of you Ann, Why?"
"I try my clothes on her to see how I look to others, Shame about the holes she cost me a lot of money."
I crouched down and felt the artery in Abbott's neck for a pulse.
"He's dead Ann; let's tie that other creep up, as you call him."
After tying him up I picked up the gun with a tissue and put it in one of the drawers.
"Better phone the police now Tom."
"Not yet Ann, as you've slept on it and as you are ready for bed the police can wait."
Ann gave me a big smile and hugged me tight. After a long kiss, she grabbed my hand and dragged me into the other bedroom slamming the door behind us.

Well, about an hour later Ann phoned the police but before they arrived we washed, dressed and then spent most of the next morning making statements to the police. The man in the doorway that killed Abbott was Simon Patterson, Abbott had lied about him being in prison to throw us off the trail; Ann was right all along about him.

Ann divorced Sid but gave him twenty-five grand as a farewell gift; Ann said it was to thank Sid for bringing me into her life. Ann is always saying nice things like that; she even bought my old flat just so we could spend our Sundays there. I've never been so happy in my life and Ann seems to get younger by the day. As for Ann being rich she had to get used to my more humble lifestyle which she loves very much. Mind you, Ann still insists we have four holidays a year together. What about the big house in the country? Well, this is the last day we will spend in it. Ann bought a cottage in Somerset and will marry me as soon as we move in and start our new life together.

Well that is how I happened to be in a big expensive house in the country. It sounds like Ann is back so I am off to give her a big hug and loads of kisses, so take care.

All the Best

Tom Logan

JAMES M DYET'S

WHITE LIES

White lies

A FRIEND IN TROUBLE AND JUST A

LITTLE WHITE LIE

THIS IS MY STORY OF HOW IT ALL BACK FIRED AND THE ADVENTURE IT SPARKED OFF.

WHITE LIES

WHITE LIES

Having decided to get out of bed early I put the television on while I got ready for work just to help me wake up, as I made my breakfast I could get the drift of what the topic on the radio was about, the guest was telling of when he told some white lies and saved the day. The moral was telling white lies are ok if they help someone. Sounded boring so I turned it off, I put one of my sixties CDs on then I carried on getting ready for work.

I set off for work, which at the time was cleaning windows on a high-rise office block from a cradle, not my first choice as a job still it paid the rent and no one ever bothered me.

I arrived at the office block and had a joke with Charlie the security man before taking the lift up to the roof, boy it was breezy up there and the cradle was swaying about, I always hated getting from the roof onto the

cradle, not a nice feeling.
After getting my equipment ready I started down the front of the building having the odd joke with the office workers at the windows as I went a really happy bunch. It was about eleven ten when I reached the Twenty third floor, which for some strange reason the architect had put a ledge round the building, the ledge protruded out about two foot which meant a rail had been put along the front of the ledge for pulleys to run along.

I tapped on the window so Tim the manager on that floor would open it and let me in through the window, it was so I could push the cradle cables onto the pulleys. Tim would always have a coffee waiting and enjoyed a chat and a few jokes, all his office staff thought the world of him and often offered a joke along with interesting topics. About eleven-forty I popped to the toilet.

As I came out of the toilet there were crying female staff and red-faced male staff looking panicky.

"It wasn't me honest, I only took a leak."
The big smile on my face soon changed when I heard a voice cry out.
"Tim's going to jump."
I rushed to the open window and looked down but saw nothing, I looked to the right and then I looked to the left, Tim was standing on the ledge about eight feet away and four feet from the corner of the building. He was holding his mobile phone to his ear and I heard him say in a desperate voice.
"You won't have to see him behind my back anymore I'm going to jump; then I will be out of your way."
He dropped his mobile phone in his top pocket and closed his eyes.
"Tim please let me talk to you before you decide to jump, please just for old time's sake."
Tim opened his eyes, looked at me and said.
"Only if you don't try to stop me, give me your word."
"You have it 100per cent Tim; I only want to talk but I want to bring the cradle along so we can talk in private, OK?"
"OK Jim I trust your word, I need to talk

to someone, I can't think straight at the moment."

As soon as I was in the cradle, I made my way along the ledge until I was in front of Tim.
"Don't worry Tim I will move the cradle if you want to jump after we have talked."
Tim's eyes were full of tears and he looked like a broken man, I was lost for words, then I smiled and said.
"It's a good thing the mother in-law got banged up last night, she was going to give me a hand today, one look at her and half of your staff would have thrown themselves out the window, so things aren't all that bad."
"Why was she arrested Jim?"
"She's a bouncer at a night club, four thugs tried to gate crash, she slammed one against the wall and knocked him out cold, kicked another in the shin with her hobnailed boot and broke his leg; she laid into the other two, blood all over the place."
"Must be self defense, why would they lock her up."
"Three big men tried to break it up and

ended up in hospital with the four thugs; problem is the three men were undercover cops looking for drugs in the club, it took four animal darts to bring her down."
Tim smiled and said.
"You're having me on Jim."
"I lied about the darts, her solicitor thinks she will get off because the cops never showed their badges, they will be off work at least three months."
Tim just smiled the same as he did when we would have our coffee, which was wonderful to see but the smile on his face soon disappeared and was replaced with a look of sadness and despair.
"What's up Tim talk to me, tell me how within five minutes you go from happy to suicidal."
"Got a phone call from a friend, they told me my wife is having an affair with one of the instructors at the gym she goes to."
"I heard what you said on your phone, what did your wife say when you phoned her."
"Someone in the office phoned my wife when I climbed out here, my wife

phoned me, when I told her why She denied having an affair but said she went to 'coffee-café' after the gym and had a coffee. As the trainer was in the coffee bar she sat at the same table."
"That was no friend that phoned you Tim; friends don't go out of their way to destroy your life. How many ladies have you sat with at lunch time and how many of them have you had an affair with; think about it Tim."
"None; never entered my head but it's not the first time that person has phoned me with news like this so what am I supposed to think."
"I don't even know your wife's name, you never talk about her."
"Her name is Pearl; her dad called her that as soon as he saw her for the first time."
"I have only known one woman called Pearl Tim, a very unusual name, where did you meet her?"
"At the Hideaway cafe in Uckfield; Pearl lived in Crowborough; her friend she knocked about with at the time is the one that phones me up, she tells me things about Pearl and the trainer."
"Crowborough is where the Pearl I used

to know came from; what road Tim?"
"Stone Cross Road, do you know it Jim.".
"It's Got to be the same one, we called her dad Jack Frost."
"Pearls dad was called Herbert, can't be the same one."
"Never knew his real name, we called him that because we called Pearl Frosty, no one ever got a kiss not even on a date, she said she was saving herself for Mr. right. Her friend was the local push bike and really got the hump when Pearl finally met; well I take it, Mr. Right was you Tim."
"Her friend Jane made out it was Pearl that slept around; mind you, her friend did look like a painted lady. Pearl was the type of girl you could take home to meet your parents."
"Have you told Pearl who has been feeding you all this poison and got her side of the story?"
"No; as far as I know Pearl has not seen or heard from Jane since we got married. I bumped into Jane in the high street, she said she would like to surprise Pearl and took my mobile number so we could fix a date."

"Why didn't you fix a date to meet Jane and how long ago did you bump into her?"
"Seven months ago but all she has done is telephone me up saying nasty things about Pearl. She even suggested that I go to her place and take her to bed. I would never do that to pearl I love her very much. I never even asked Jane where she lived and haven't seen her since the high street."
"What are you doing on that ledge Tim, you must know it's all a pack of lies Jane's been feeding you, why do you have doubts about Pearl."
"She has been seen with that instructor once in a wine bar in town, his name is Jeff Thomas, and Pearl has his phone number on her mobile phone."

Sue; Tim's secretary shouted out the window.
"Tim your wife is on her way up in the lift, please don't jump."
"Your looking a bit pale Tim do you want to clime into the cradle incase you pass out, you can always chuck yourself off later, have it out with your wife first."

Tim looked more scared of facing his wife than he did standing 23 floors up on the ledge, he put his hand out for me to help him into the cradle, which I did and then we made our way back to the window.
Tim called out. “Pearl!” In surprise as his wife leaned out the widow to help him in.
“I think you two should go into Tim’s office and have a talk.”
I said as Tim slid over the window ledge into the office. Tim fell into Pearls arms ending with a long embrace and after Pearl gave Tim a big kiss and told him she loved him, Pearl turned to me as I climbed in and said.
“It can’t be; it is; Jim do you remember me? Little miss frosty; you have not changed a bit, still Mr. lonely heart are you? You were the shy one, fancy seeing you again after all this time.”
I stood there in shock; everything I had said to Tim about Pearl was a pack of white lies just to get him to come in off the ledge. Now a woman I have never met in my life is making me think it was all true. No one could have heard what we were talking about and Pearl was

not even in the building when I was making it all up.

Tim and Pearl went into Tim's office and closed the door, as the door closed cheers and clapping came from the staff, to my embarrassment it was for me for getting Tim back in, so red faced I headed for the window to carry on my work.

I carried on working till it was time to knock off which was about four thirty and after putting everything away I went down in the lift; I said goodbye to Charlie the security guard who handed me a sealed envelope. I put in my inside pocket and went home.

When I got home I poured myself a double whisky and sat down to relax for a while. I must have dozed off because next thing I knew it was eight o'clock, I got up and made some cheese on toast. Later I remembered the letter and thinking it could be my P45, with dread I opened it only to find it was from Pearl, she was inviting me to dinner on this coming Sunday with her and Tim.

The week went quickly and I was starting to feel a little anxious about the whole business, even my white lies seem to have backfired on me, I consoled myself that at least Tim was alive. Well it is Sunday morning and I am all spruced up and ready to leave for Tim's house for dinner I took a deep breath then headed out the door.

When I arrived at Tim and Pearls house a man with a rather angry look on his face came towards me up the path from Tim's front door.
"Are they in?"
I asked the man as he reached me.
"You're Jim I take it; you have ruined everything, get out of my way."
The man rushed past and disappeared out the gate. Suddenly I felt like the bad guy, I wonder who he was. Everybody seems to know me yet I don't know any of them, I felt like I must be living through one of those weird dreams, yet no it's all real.

I reached the front door and pressed the doorbell which sounded like Big Ben going off, then the door opened

and there stood Pearl wearing a soft pink pleated skirt and white cotton blouse with pink high heal shoes to match.
“You look very attractive Pearl; Tim’s a very lucky man.”
“Thanks Jim; Tim’s out on the patio so go through and help your self to a drink on the way.”
“Could you tell me who that man was that left as I arrived?”
“That was Jeff from the gym; He came round to see if I wanted to go for a jog with him, what a cheek!”
“He wasn’t very happy and seemed to think I had messed everything up for him, he didn’t say what and I haven’t a clue what he meant.”
“I will tell you more when we get a chance to be alone Jim.”
“Does Tim know he called?”
“No! Please don’t mention he’s been to the house.”
“Ok I will grab a drink and find Tim.”
After pouring myself a whisky I found Tim sitting at the garden table which was a rather smart silver and gold trimmed wooden table with chairs to match, the gold matched Tim’s pint of

larger perfectly.
"Hello Tim how are you feeling?"
"Feeling better today, sorry for the trouble I caused yesterday, I feel such an idiot, thanks for coming Jim."
"All forgotten about Tim but your staff have nailed all the windows shut and put shackles and chains on your office chair."
Tim just gave a big smile and had a drink of his lager. I sat in one of the chairs opposite Tim, as he sipped his lager I could see he was deep in thought and had a stern look on his face, he stared into space.
"Penny for your thoughts Tim; a problem shared is a problem halved as they say."
"Wish it was that simple Jim, I will tell you when we are alone as someone might be in earshot."
Talk about piggy in the middle, both Pearl and Tim want to tell me something without the other hearing. How did I get in this mess, I hate all this secrecy. Pearl shouted from the window.
"Tim the wine, where is it?"
"I thought you were getting it when you

went shopping yesterday, have we run out already?"
"Yes we have, could you pop out and get some before the dinner is ready and before you have too much to drink."
"Ok; how many bottles of red wine do we need darling?"
"Three should be enough, thank you Tim and don't be long."
Tim gave a sigh; He had another drop of his lager got up and headed back into the house.
"Did you want me to go with you Tim?" I asked.
"No I won't be long, help yourself to another drink."
Tim disappeared down the hall shortly followed by the sound of the front door slamming.

I sat in the garden chair wondering if it was a good idea to have accepted the dinner invitation. Pearl appeared at the patio door, she asked if I would like to have dinner outside in the garden or in the dinning room and would I like another drink.
"I would like a coffee if that's ok, lovely place you have here."

“I love it Jim, I’m really happy here and so is Tim, if only people would leave us alone, not much to ask is it?”
“Did you settle this problem with Tim? He still looks troubled.”
“I don’t think he believes me, if he knew Jeff had called at the house that would be the last straw; he would probably think Jeff had been calling while he was at work.”
“What did you say to Jeff when he called? It must have been a bit of a shock when you opened the front door and saw him standing there.”
“I told him he had to find someone else to talk to about his women problems, as it was causing problems for me and I am not going to the gym anymore.”
“That’s what Jeff meant when he said I had ruined everything, but how am I responsible for you not seeing Jeff anymore, seems strange.”
“He approached me in the first place and asked my advice over the strange behavior of his lady friend and asked how he could make her fall for him.”
“Sounds more like he wanted you to tell him how to make you fall for him by telling him you’re secret likes and

dislikes."
"I don't know Jim, why would he be after me? There are lots of younger women at the gym and they are more his own age; he has his girl friend he seems to be in love with."
"Have you seen his girl friend?"
"No, I don't even know her name, he asked me for advise on what women want from a man and what turned women on, he said he is desperately in love with her and thought he was losing her, he thought I knew how he could make her fall for him."
"I suppose you told him what turned you on and what you like in a man, thinking it would be the same for his girl friend."
"Your right I did, how stupid of me."

There was a bang as the front door slammed shut; Tim had arrived home with the wine, I started to talk to Pearl about my job just to change the subject. Tim came straight in and gave Pearl a kiss, then asked us if we were talking over old times.
"Old times are better left in the past, just telling Pearl what a good bunch of people work at the office block."

“Hope your not letting all our secrets out Jim?”
“I can’t think of any at the moment Tim.”
“Fancy having a bite to eat out here in the garden or would you rather eat indoors you two.”
Pearl asked in a rather cheerful voice.
“What do you think Jim?” asked Tim.
“I’m easy, I don’t mind.”
“Better watch you with Pearl if you’re that easy then.”
Tim said and grinned.
“Any more of those remarks and I will tell Pearl about you and that secretary with that cough and big boobs.”
Tim looked at me with a puzzled look on his face.
“What secretary.”
“You said she was chesty, so she slapped you’re face.”
Tim looked even more puzzled and a bit red in the face. Pearl laughed and gave Tim a kiss then said.
“One of Jim’s jokes darling you should see your face.”
Then she gave him a hug. Tim looked at me, grinned and said.
“Next time you come thorough the window you can have hot chocolate

laced with laxative."
"I think I will bring my flask, it's safer."
By this time, Pearl had declared we would all go in for lunch and then come back out in the garden for drinks after lunch.

The meal was delicious, a good Sunday dinner with all the vegetables, roast spuds and to my amazement a meat free roast.
"Hope you don't mind Jim we don't eat meat, hope you like it."
"I don't eat meat either, lovely gravy Pearl."
"It's Bisto I always use it, there's no animal derivatives."
Pearl said a satisfied look on her face.
"Is there anything you're not good at Pearl." I asked.
"Keeping my man happy, I can't seem to get that right."
All went silent and we all carried on eating, I never looked up until I had finished eating then said.
"Thank you both for a lovely meal, I haven't had a meal like that for years, I forgot how good it was."
"Come on let's go and have some wine

out in the garden and Tim you get the glasses, Jim you can bring the tray of cakes and biscuits, let's make the most of the Sun."

The rest of the day went off with no more jokes and a there was a nice restful atmosphere, about six pm I stood up and said.
"Well you lovely people what can I say, except what a wonderful day, thank you both very much."
"You sure you have to go Jim? We've enjoyed your company." Tim asked.
"Got work in the morning, not looking forward to that hot chocolate though."
"Think we will stick to coffee Jim it's safer."
Pearl gave me a peck on the cheek and Tim shook my hand, he thanked me for everything I had done and I set off home.

The next day I was back to work and when I reached Tim's floor my cup of coffee was waiting as usual; Tim looked back to his old cheerful self.
"You ok Tim? You're looking a bit more like the Tim we're used to today."

"Feel a lot better thanks, mind you that Jane phoned but I never answered, bet she tries again later."
"Tell you what Tim, tell her you want to meet her at her flat."
"You must be joking, why would I want to do that?"
"To find out her address then I will go and have a word with her, I will go in your place what do you think?"
"Try anything just to get her off my back; it would be great if you could."
"Arrange it for this Saturday afternoon Tim, say two pm."
"Ok, are you sure you don't mind? "
"Be a pleasure Tim, well I had better get back to those windows."

The week seemed to go quite slowly but finally Saturday arrived. Tim had given me the address, flat four Sunnyside court, Sycamore Street. I looked and was surprised to find it was three streets from where I lived. I decided I would get there half an hour early and practice what I would say.

When I arrived at the street I walked along looking at the lovely blossom trees lining each side of the road, as I glanced up the street I spotted Jeff Thomas from the gym walk out of a driveway. Mr. Thomas never looked my way as he walked in the opposite direction, as I got to the driveway he had came out of I noticed it was Sunnyside court. Feeling a bit confused I decided to call on Jane now, my watch said it was 1.40pm so it was not too early. I walked into the main porch and noticed the main door was ajar; I ignored the doorbell as I thought it would be easier to explain face to face.

Flat four was what I would describe as an attic flat right at the top of some steep stairs, they resembled the type you see on a ship and they wound round to the right and up to Jane's front door. Feeling a bit out of breath when I reached the top of the stairs I waited until I got my breath back, I knocked on Jane's door taking care not to step back as there was only two feet between the top stairs and the door. I heard a noise inside then the door opened and to my amazement a

woman of about 5ft, slim and wearing a light green-buttoned cardigan, cream blouse and cream slacks with one of the prettiest, sweetest faces I had ever seen appeared in the doorway.
"Can I help you?"
She said in a faint sweet voice.
"Did someone let you in or has someone left the door open again?"
"The door was ajar so I came straight up; my name is James Matthews, I have come in Tim's place, can I come in and talk to you please?"
Without saying a word Jane backed away from the door with her right palm up in front of her as if she was scared I had come to hurt her.
"I only want to talk Jane, you are Tim and pearls friend are you not?"
She stared at me with an angry look in her eyes then said. "Come in."
Tears started to run down her cheeks. Before I could step through the door I felt a thud on the back of my neck and a terrific pain shoot up into my head, the room went blurred and the floor zoomed up to my eyes as I sunk to my knees, as I brought my head up to look at Jane I heard a loud bang, through my blurred

vision I could see Jane swaying about and a red stain slowly running down her slacks. Without thinking I grabbed the door frame with both hands, then with all my strength shot to my feet, I went reeling backwards and I remember my back hitting something before I pulled my self into the room, I staggered forward towards Jane, I could see she was about to fall over; by this time it had sunk in that she had been shot, I grabbed hold of Jane to try to break her fall; I did but fell over myself as my dizziness was getting worse; The next thing I knew was a tugging at my hair and Jane's voice asking me to phone for an ambulance, I rolled over on my front and slowly got to my feet, Jane was lying on her side crying and as I kneeled down beside her I saw her blouse and slacks covered in blood, I squeezed her shoulder then went to her phone and called for an ambulance. I told Jane I would have to try to stop the blood and she nodded, I undone her cardigan and blouse and could see a dark red hole just under her collarbone. I picked up a tea towel off the ironing board and pressed it on the hole which

seemed to stop the flow of blood, at least I hoped it had; I looked at Jane lying there frightened and still crying and I was lost for words, perhaps for the first time in my life. I took the throw off the settee and covered Jane up as she would have lost a lot of body heat after losing all that blood, I knelt back down and pressed on the wound again, Jane looked up at me and squeezed my hand then said.
"Thank you I have forgotten your name already, good thing you came when you did I feel really cold."
"My name is James Matthew's, call me Jim, did you see who did this?"
"No because I had started crying and put my right hand over my eyes, I heard the shot then felt the pain, all I saw was you swaying about in the doorway."

It seemed ages before the ambulance arrived but they quickly dealt with Jane and looked very professional. As they put Jane on the stretcher two police officers walked through the door and said to the ambulance men.
"Don't move anything, including her."

One of the ambulance men, a rather big burly man stood up looked at the police and said.
"Try and stop us you moron."
The police officer went red in the face and moved to one side to let the men out the door. The police officers looked at me and asked what had gone on here, I told them in a rather garbled way as I was still light headed, with what I can only describe as the worst hangover I have ever had.
"Wait! I remembered bumping into something as I swung backwards in the doorway after the shot rang out, I must have knocked the intruder down the stairs."

I went to the door and slowly made my way down the stairs looking for clues as I went, about halfway down the stairs I found a lens out of a pair of spectacles and at the bottom of the flight of stairs I found what looked like a tooth with blood on it. I never touched either, I just called the police and they said the forensic team was on the way, they suggested they take me to hospital as I kept swaying about and suggested I may have concussion.

The police took me to the hospital and when the doctor examined me she said that they would keep me in for the night. The police said they would pop back tomorrow morning to see me.
I asked the nurse in casualty were I was supposed to sleep for the night; she smiled and said.
"Nowhere for the next two hours."
As it was only four twenty in the afternoon and it would be better to stay awake after a blow to the head that did not seem too much of a problem even though I felt tired.

As there were two hospitals in the town I walked over to reception and asked if they had admitted a woman with a gunshot wound, .
"Are you her husband? I believe you were with her when it happened."
"I was, I thought she was single, what makes you think she's married."
"The lady referred to herself as Mrs. Jane Swift."
"Have you any news how she is? She

lost a lot of blood."
"The doctors say she will be ok, I will see if a doctor can have a word with you after he's asked Mrs. Swift's permission of course."

It must have been over an hour before anyone came to talk to me, then a young surgeon turned up still in his Wellington's etc, he had a big smile on his face and said.
"How is the headache now any better?"
"Not really but I thought you had news of Mrs. Swift."
"Thanks to you stopping the blood loss when you did she should be ok, luckily the bullet didn't do too much damage and missed the bone."
"When can I see her? I need to talk to her before the police come back tomorrow."
"Your still a bit groggy at present but I believe you will be sharing a private room together till the other police come back tomorrow."
"What do you mean other police?"
"A plain clothed police man has been around since she arrived and will be outside the room all night."

“Any chance of some pain killers I’ve got a really bad headache?”
“Follow me I will show you your room and get a nurse to bring you some tablets.”

We arrived at the room then the surgeon looked at the back of my head to assess the damage.
“Not much of a bump but a big bruise looks more like soft tissue damage.”
“Does that mean no concussion?”
“That’s right but the police still want to keep you here for the night, although it’s not concussion you will still get dizzy spells and headaches, because the nerves to your face and head come out of the vertebra in your neck.”
The nurse turned up about ten minutes later with the tablets and asked if I would like a cup of tea or coffee and perhaps a couple of biscuits.
“Black coffee one and a half sugars please.” I replied.
The coffee and biscuits and tablets were soon consumed then I fell asleep.

When I woke up Jane was on the other bed looking very pale and sad.

"Jane, how are you feeling? I'm glad you're going to be ok."
"You're finally awake, so boring with no one to talk to, at least you don't snore Jim that's one blessing."
"I forgot to tell the police I saw a man called Jeff Thomas leaving your flats as I was walking towards your driveway."
"Please don't tell them Jim, please."
"Do you know him Jane, why don't you want to tell the police, he could be the one who shot you?"
"No it would not be Jeff, hope it's not who I think it might be."
"How can you be so sure it was not Jeff, I don't trust him?"
"He's my brother he's been helping me."
"Helping you do what? He's trying to get off with Tim's wife, Pearl."
"It's not what you think Jim, believe me."
"All I know is Jeff and you are trying to destroy their marriage."
Jane started to cry and said.
"You don't understand I can't say anymore please don't think badly of me, I was wrong to try."
"I never meant to upset you Jane, still who ever shot you lost a lens out of their glasses and a tooth, I accidentally

knocked the person down your steep stairs."
"Jeff doesn't wear glasses so that should eliminate him, you see."
"Well nothing makes sense to me, are you shielding someone?"
"Drop it Jim and leave well alone, I don't know if I can trust you yet."
"The police will want to know, don't forget the killer knows you're still alive."
"What are you saying don't frighten me."
"Who ever shot you wants you dead and may try again."
"I don't know who would want to kill me or why."
"Your very attractive, you can have anyone you want, why Tim? He is a nice man but not that good looking and not exactly rich."
"You haven't got a clue Jim you don't know him."
I started to get a bit annoyed and raised my voice.
"We're going round in circles, why don't you just spit it out."

The door flew open and a plain clothed policeman rushed in and stared at both of us; he asked what was going

on as he heard raised voices.
"Sorry it's this blinding headache it's getting on top of me; can you go and ask the nurse for some tablets?"
"I will, I'll be back in a minute."
The plain clothed police officer disappeared down the corridor.
"What ever happens is down to you Jane and your big secret."
I put my jacket on and started out the door.
"Jim, where are you going?"
"To find out some answers, all of you have taken me for an idiot."

I went straight to the gym and looked around until I found Jeff; I walked up to him and said.
"Your sister Jane is dead! Any ideas on who could have shot her?"
Jeff stared at me then said.
"Jane can't be, I saw her this afternoon she was fine and how did you know I was Jane's brother?"
"Jane told me but she wouldn't tell me what you two are up to."

Just then a shot rang out, blood ran down Jeff's temple and he dropped

like a stone to the floor, I looked round and saw no one, I felt Jeff's neck for a pulse and found one it looked like the bullet had skimmed his temple; I phoned the police and told them that I was talking to Jeff when it happened.
I waited with Jeff then cleared off when I saw them arrive. I wondered what was going on and then it suddenly came back into my mind about Pearl backing up my white lies! Must find out how she did that.

I arrived at Pearls and Tim's house about six thirty and rang the doorbell then waited, the door opened and there stood Pearl.
"Hello Jim what are you doing here did you forget something?"
"Give me a big smile Pearl, it's very important."
Without hesitating Pearl gave one of her lovely smiles, exposing all her lovely white teeth all still intact.
"Can I come in pearl I really need to talk to some one I can trust?"
Pearl beckoned me in and I followed her to the kitchen.
"Want a coffee Jim? Don't worry I know

how you like it."
"Thank you Pearl, I am completely lost to what's going on."
I told Pearl everything about Jane and Jeff; she seemed even more confused than I was.
"Tim not home from work yet Pearl?"
"Tim has had to go to a meeting in Maidstone; He won't be back till next week sometime, is it important you talk to him?"
"All I have are questions and no answers Pearl; do you know this Jane and Jeff think carefully?"
"Sorry Jim, never heard of Jane and I only know Jeff through the Gym club, sorry about Jeff and his sister."
"I think the shootings are somehow connected with you two."
"Not me Jim but why did Tim not say about this Jane."
"I think the burning question is, how did you know that I called you Miss Frosty, I really would like to know."
"When I phoned Tim he dropped the mobile in his top pocket without turning it off, I heard every word you two said."
"Tim must have gone along with it as well, I feel such an idiot, why would he

do that?"
"Did this Jane say why her and her brother is trying to break us up? What could be their motif, it seems very strange."
"The answer lies with Jane, why would she not tell me it's so annoying."
"Perhaps if you had another word with Jane she may tell you now her brother has been shot as well."
I started towards the door then stopped and remarked.
"I only saw Tim this morning strange he never said about the meeting, a bit sudden, when did he tell you?"
"Tim phoned me about two thirty, it was rather odd especially on a Saturday I hope he is not involved."
As Pearl spoke everything went blurred and I felt light headed, next thing I felt an arm round my waist and heard Pearl.
"Jim what's wrong? Come and sit down before you fall."
Pearl held onto me until I got to the armchair, I slumped backwards into the armchair and passed out.

When I came to I was still in the armchair with a blanket over me, the room was in semi darkness and just a table lamp was on at the other end of the room. I glanced around then heard voices so I stayed where I was waiting for them to finish. I could make out two voices Pearls and another woman's voice; the other woman voice had a nasty tone to it and shouting angrily. Pearl sounded confused then started to scream.

I quickly got out the chair and rushed to the doorway, I could see a woman with her back to me and Pearl was about eight feet in front of the woman looking terrified.
Pearl spotted me and shouted.
"She has a gun."
I rushed towards the woman and as she turned I saw the gun; I was right on top of the woman before she had turned far enough round to fire the gun; I crashed into her in a badly executed rugby tackle sending her and myself sprawling across the room. I came to a full stop against the front of the settee and quickly got to my feet, I looked around the room and to my amazement I spotted the woman disappearing out the

living room door, as I went to give chase I noticed Pearl pointing the gun at me. I looked at Pearl who had a strange look on her face, neither of us moved or spoke for a few seconds then pearl lowered the gun dropped it to the floor and started crying.
I went over to pearl who seemed to be in shock, I took her in my arms which brought on an even bigger flood of tears, then she put her arms around me and asked what was going on.

After a few minutes Pearl had calmed down a bit, I went and locked all the doors and windows in case the woman came back, Pearl asked for a gin and tonic and I had a double whisky. We sat down had a few sips of our drinks then I asked Pearl what the woman was talking to her about.
"She said I stole her husband and she has made sure I would not get their son and daughter; she said when Tim gets home she will shoot him, that's when you appeared at the door."
"Has Tim ever mentioned a son and daughter or that he had been married before?"

"No, he told me I was his first serious relationship, the woman must be mistaken and she said she had killed his son and daughter, she must have been talking about Jeff and Jane."
"I think its time to phone the police Pearl perhaps they can throw some light on the subject."

After phoning the police who just told us to lock all the doors and windows till they got there I got Pearl a second glass of Gin and Tonic and put it on the coffee table in front of her.
"Just got to pop to the toilet Pearl, it's just down the hall as I remember."
"No that one is out of order, when you came to dinner Tim got drunk after you left and broke the handle off the cistern, use the one in the bedroom on the right at the top of the stairs."

I started up the stairs thinking how lucky they were to have such a lovely place, I put the bedroom light on then went into the en suit bathroom, I put the light on then shut the door. Afterwards as I opened the bathroom door I noticed the bedroom light was off and by the

light of the bathroom I could make out a woman's figure by the bed swaying her hips from side to side.
"We should have stuck to one drink pearl, come on lets get something to eat I'm starving and the police should be here soon."
I walked over to the swaying figure but as I got close I could make out that their hair was long, Pearls hair was shoulder length, before I could do anything the figure lunged forward and I felt an agonizing pain in my left arm, I instinctively pushed the figure away and as it came at me again I punched it as hard as I could in the face then got out of the bedroom door and shut it behind me.
"Pearl! Come here quick and bring the gun, hurry."
I shouted as I made my way down the stairs, as I reached the bottom Pearl appeared with the gun, she was looking rather concerned.
"Jim what's the matter? You have my tin opener sticking in your arm, she's still in the house isn't she?"
"Keep the gun pointed at the bedroom door and shoot her if she comes out, I

feel a bit sick, good job it missed the bone, look! I got it out, boy that hurts I can feel the blood running down my arm."

"Can you hold the gun so I can get a bandage?"

"Be a pleasure Pearl, don't be long or you will have a bloody carpet."

Pearl rushed off to the kitchen and soon returned with her first aid box and bandaged my arm.

"I think I must have knocked her out, I'm sure it is the same woman that had the gun, long hair and smelling of moth balls."

About twenty minutes went by; we stayed at the bottom of the stairs with the gun at the ready when there was a knock on the door.

"About time the police got here, can you let them in Pearl?"

Pearl made her way to the front door, which was opposite the bottom of the stairs and opened it.

"Jim!" Pearl Shouted as she quickly slammed the door shut. As the door shut four metal prongs protruded through the middle of the door panel and started moving about, just as if the

person was trying to pull them back out.
"It's her! She's got a garden fork, shoot her! Shoot her through the door Jim! What are you waiting for?"
"I've noticed there is only one bullet in the gun, I can't take a chance on wasting it."
"Phone the police again Jim, please phone them."
"Come on let's stick together and watch each others back."
I said as I backed away from the menacing front door.

I phoned the police and told them what had just happened, they told me a patrol car was on its way and should be there anytime now, they said they would phone the patrol car and then phone me back.
"Our drinks are still here, just what we need."
"Good idea, I could do with a good drink, this is like a nightmare Jim."
We heard a car screech to a halt and shouting from outside then came a knock on the door.
"Who is it?"
Pearl asked in a trembling voice.

"It's me Tim, what's that garden fork doing stuck in the door? Open the door and let me in."
I put my hand on Pearls shoulder and moved her away from the door, I stood to the side of the front door with the gun, I nodded for Pearl to open the door which she did, then took two paces back. There stood Tim looking rather annoyed and Red in the face.
"Well what's going on why are you pointing that gun at me?"
"I think you're the one that's got the explaining to do."
Just then a police officer came to the door, he told us two of his men are in chase of a woman waving a swap hook about, I asked if I could give him the gun for safekeeping, he nodded and took it, we all sat down and told Tim and the police what had happened. Tim sat there deep in thought.
"Well Tim what's all this about? I'm your wife I have a right to know."
"The woman is Susan Tad, I lodged with her when I worked in the midlands years before we met, we became very close in fact to close, she became insanely jealous to the point she

followed me to work or sent Jeff or Jane to spy on me."
"So they are your children Tim, why didn't you tell me?"
"They looked on me as their Dad; Susan had been in a bad relation ship with their father, he had cleared off months before I arrived, Susan was very attractive at the time and wanted me to marry her, I told her from the start I never wanted a serious relationship but Susan tried to stab me when I refused the second time, that's when I left.
I waited until she took the kids to see a friend; I packed and left her a note. The children were only about four at the time, I never recognized them."
Another policeman came in to let us know that the woman had been apprehended and locked in the police car. The police left and Tim and Pearl ran me to the hospital to have my arm looked at.

We learned the next day that Susan had met someone after Tim left, she suffered beatings from the man who tried to rape Jane and he put Jeff in intensive care for trying to stop him. Susan blamed Tim; if he hadn't left none of this would have happened. When Susan found out Tim had married Pearl her deranged mind looked on it as bigamy. She recognized Tim from the sports club, Susan thought he was going to take Jeff away from her. Susan sent Jane to try to break up Tim's marriage and when it failed she decided to kill you, Jeff, Jane and herself.

Susan was taken to a prison hospital for treatment. Jeff stayed on at the club and Jane, well! We are on our honeymoon; I just hope she doesn't turn out like her mother.
Tim and Pearl decided to go away for a while and booked a two-week holiday in Greece. When they returned Jeff and Jane visited Tim regularly and Jane confided in me that they still looked on Tim as their dad. This one white lie gave me a lot of pain but it also gave me the woman of my dreams.

All the best

James Matthews

James M Dyet's

WHY ME

WHY ME

It was just an ordinary Friday and everything seemed fine.

Then whatever I did went wrong until I seemed to have lost everything including my wife daughter and mother-in law all in one weekend.

WHY ME?

Hi my name is Tim Short, I suppose you have had the odd nightmare just like everyone else, But how many have you had while awake?

Let me tell you about mine and how I was driven to near suicide. I have always thought of myself as a considerate husband and father and I have a lovely devoted wife and a wonderful five year old daughter Susan, yes I love them very much. I work for myself as a builder handyman so there is never much free time to spend with my family; well that's what it seemed at the time.

It was July the 25th when my life changed, it was a lovely sunny day and we were all happy when I left for work. Sally my wife and Daughter Susan were going to spend the day at Sally's mothers and I was off to hang some roller blinds for a customer.

I set off in my van but only got half way to my destination when I was flagged down by an old gentleman who was staggering in the road, I thought he was drunk to start with but his dog had pulled him over and ran off.
“Please help me I have to find my dog, I’m afraid he will get hurt, please help!”
Looking in the direction the man was pointing I noticed a Jack Russell cocking its leg against a signpost; the dog was about fifty yards away down the road, keeping an eye on the dog I walked with a quick pace towards it; as I got about ten feet away from the dog it started walking away, after following the dog past about five houses the dog stopped and stared at another dog in a garden giving me chance to grab his lead. I reached the old man with the reluctant dog, he thanked me and the happy old man disappeared with his dog.

Feeling pleased with myself I got back in my van and started the engine, I heard a loud bang as a car sped past only to find my wing mirror gone, I picked it up from the road and slung it in the back of the van.

What crossed my mind was, if I hadn't stopped to help catch the dog this would never have happened. Still the dog was safe and the old chap was happy and off home with his best friend.

I carried on through the town only to find a new speed camera had been put up. This I noticed for the first time when it flashed at me. "More expense".

Finally I arrived at my first job and grabbing my toolbox from the back of the van I pulled it out, only to find the catches undone and my tools shot across the road. Before I could retrieve them a lorry drove passed and ran over them. I retrieved them and found the only things usable was the hammer, a Starred screwdriver and side cutters, with the odd tools the lady had and what was left of mine I completed the job. The money I was paid all went on replenishing some of my toolbox. I set off to the petrol station only to find I had left my wallet at home.

I arrived home and went upstairs to the bedroom. Picking up my wallet from my bedside cabinet I noticed one of the windows had been left open. Feeling in a bad mood I slammed it shut, this made a length of guttering swing down pass the window smashing through the middle of the green house roof, I sat on the edge of the bed feeling near to tears, I was hoping this was just a horrible nightmare and I would soon wake up.

I set off to get some petrol and then to my next job and to my delight I arrived without further incidents. Farmer Joe wanted one of his five bar gates mending, what could go wrong on the edge of a field? Nothing! How wrong I was, while I had the gate open the sheep decided to escape. I tried to stop the sheep and just got head butted out of the way. I phoned the farmer and lost about 40 minute's helping the farmer round them up. By the time I finished the gate the morning was gone.

I left and went to the local stockist's for my make of car and had the wing mirror replaced. This left me with £70.50p for a mornings work.

Feeling fed up I went home and made myself some beans on toast and a big cup of black coffee. As I hadn't got any more jobs lined up for the rest of the day I decided to mend the guttering.

After mending the gutter I thought I had better do something with the greenhouse, all I could find was a sheet of tarpaulin and after a struggle I managed to put it over the roof of the greenhouse and by this time I felt tired, I just felt like a sit down and have forty winks. As I started to doze off in the armchair the telephone rang, it was my wife Sally letting me know she would be late as they were having dinner and tea at her mothers.

As I put the receiver back down it rang again, this time a woman who had seen my add in the local shop wanted me to assemble a wardrobe she had just purchased. Feeling great at the thought of a nice easy money earner I set off.

As I arrived at the property I could see that the lady was well off, she had a big four-wheel drive on the drive and the

detached house and grounds had been well maintained. I pressed the doorbell and heard what sounded like Alsatians barking fiercely from inside and feeling apprehensive I got back in the van and watched to see what emerged.
The door opened and a woman stood in the doorway wearing a track suit, she beckoned to me so I got out the van and went over.
"Don't worry that's just my door bell, certainly fooled you Mr Short."
"It sounds very realistic and very loud."
"The delivery men have put the flat pack wardrobe upstairs in the bedroom, let me show you and then I will make you a drink if you would like one?"
"Very kind perhaps a black coffee with one and a half spoons of sugar."
"My name is Jean Day, what's yours?"
"My name is Tim."
And with that I followed the lady upstairs.
I felt my lower jaw drop when I saw the size of the stack of boxes.
"I don't think I will be able to complete all that today but I can make a start."

“That’s fine I will get your coffee and let you get started.”

The bedroom was a good-sized room with plenty of room to work and by the size of the pile of boxes the wardrobe would cover an entire wall. I opened the boxes containing the bases, solid oak, must have cost a fortune.
“Here is your coffee Tim I will put it on my dresser.”
“Thank you Mrs Day, love your choice of wood.”
“Call me Jean please, it certainly cost enough but I fell in love with it.”
“Thank you for the coffee I will carry on and get as much done as I can today.”
“No rush! Just take your time, I will go and get changed.”

I completed about a third of the wardrobe when Mrs Day appeared in the room wearing a skirt, blouse, sparkling necklace and her face made up.
“Leave that for now Tim I ordered a big pizza for us and it’s just arrived, come on before it gets cold.”
As I rose to my feet I could feel my self-

tremble as I gazed at Mrs Day, slim, long black hair and a smile that made you melt.
"Don't worry Tim I am expecting my boyfriend later he's taking me out."
"Thanks for putting my mind at rest Mrs Day, sorry I mean Jean, for the moment I thought, well you know!"
"Yes I was flattered to see the expression on your face, I wish I had had my camera with me."

After we consumed The Pizza which was delicious I looked at my watch.
"I will have to get home but I will be back early to try and get the wardrobe finished, what time is best?"
"Best make it about nine thirty, I may have a late night depending on what John has planned and if he spends the night, best if I give you a ring first."
"Ok I will see you tomorrow I will do one of my other jobs first so call me on my mobile number on this card."

As I drove out the drive a black BMW turned into the drive, the man driving glared at me as he passed, he looked an arrogant looking man in his forties with

greased back hair and a silly looking moustache.
When I arrived home my wife and daughter were watching a film so I joined them on the settee and told Sally about my day.

I was awoken the next morning by a very angry Sally poking my shoulder.
"What's going on Tim? There's a woman called Jean on the phone crying she said she needs you to go to her as soon as you can."
I was speechless; I sat there shrugging my shoulders.
"Well! I want to know what's going on, answer me."
"I told you I was putting a wardrobe together for a woman called Jean Day; nothing is going on she has a boyfriend and he arrived as I left."
"Perhaps she has other ideas on what she wants from you Timothy."
Sally only called me by my full Christian name when she was really annoyed.
"Let's drop Susan off to school and you can come and help me at Mrs Day's."
"I think that's a good idea at least I won't

be driving myself mad wondering what you're up to."
We dropped Susan off at her school and drove to Mrs Day's.

We arrived at Mrs Day's and sally remarked what a lovely place it was.
Mrs Day opened the front door looking really upset and worried.
"What's up Mrs Day? By the way this is my wife Sally, she's come to help."
"Follow me up to my bedroom."
Sally stared at me with a straight cold look as we followed Mrs Day upstairs.
As we entered the bedroom we were greeted by parts of the wardrobe strewn over the room, the part of the wardrobe I had assembled was lying on its side.
"Don't tell me Mrs Day you had a quarrel with your boyfriend?"
"We will not be having anymore I have finished with him for good."
"Did he think something was going on between you and my husband?"
"Good heavens no, he wanted to borrow some money, I said I couldn't let him have any due to the expense of the wardrobe."

Sally and I looked at each other and smiled a sigh of relief, then we started to tidy the room up, after putting the part I had assembled upright.
"Believe it or not nothing is damaged good job its solid oak."
"Sorry about all this Mrs Short, would you like to give me a hand to make us all a drink, I will pay you the same as your husband as you're giving him a hand."
"Please call me Sally and call him Mr Short, Only joking its Tim."
"My name is Jean. Let's get the kettle on."

I started putting the wardrobe together, Sally appeared about ten minutes later with my coffee and she smiled then disappeared. I never saw Sally again until later after I had finished the wardrobe.

I found them both sitting in the kitchen talking and laughing.
"I've finished have a look and see what you think?"
Excitedly Jean rushed upstairs followed by Sally and myself and then came cries of joy echoing from Mrs Day.
"Its wonderful thank you, thank you so

much."
"Glad you like it, I think it's lovely, a beautiful piece of furniture." I remarked.
"Let me make you both some dinner before you go."
"Sorry we have to pick our daughter up from school, thanks anyway."
As we left Jean handed me an envelope and thanked us again. The envelope contained two hundred pounds which we split down the middle.

After picking Susan up from school we decided to go and splash out on a meal. Sally said she new a lovely new restaurant, it had been recommended by one of the mothers at the school. Sally wanted to try it so that's where we went.

When we ordered Sally wanted to make it special by having a bottle of Champaign with the meal. At last things were going right, my luck had changed. We all enjoyed the meal feeling very happy, that was until I had the bill handed to me. The cost of the meal was £37 and to my horror, fifty-three pounds for the champagne, this left me with about £10 for one and a half days work. I didn't want to spoil the meal for Sally and Susan so I paid up and kept quite.

Sally blew her top when she saw the greenhouse, then she apologised as it was not my fault. I never had the nerve to say it was because I had slammed the window shut. Feeling really down I went to bed to have an early night leaving the girls watching a soppy DVD film. I had snuggled down and was drifting off into a lovely sleep when I was awoken by Susan shouting.
"The electricity has gone, hurry dad."
Reluctantly I put my slippers on and made my way to the garage to reset the RCD on the fuse box. Just my luck, the heavens opened up soaking me before I could get back indoors. I decided to have a hot bath before putting on dry cloths and going to bed, only to be told by Sally that she had used all the hot water from the emersion heater and forgot to put it on again. I just dried myself and went back to bed cold.

Next morning Sally woke me with a cup of tea, feeling pleased I sat up and took

a swig.
"Sally! What have you put in the tea? It tastes funny and it's made me sweat."
"Sorry I must have got the sugar muddled up with the salt."
"I think I will make my own, still thanks for the thought sweetheart."
She went red in the face and shouted.
"Please yourself! Do you want me to throw your cheese on toast away too?"
I never answered, I knew once a woman takes that tone you're heading for a blazing row, I just shook my head and never made eye contact.

After breakfast I changed and got the van out ready to take Susan to school, I went back in and asked if Susan was up and getting ready as she would be late for school, Sally glared at me.
"Are you deliberately trying to annoy me today? There's no school on Saturday's."
Feeling even more depressed I just turned and left without speaking and headed for one of my jobs I had lined up.

Mrs Anna Tyler was a regular customer, I got the idea she created jobs to

get me round there for company, Eighty five years old and one of the dearest souls I have ever met. The kitchen cupboard was the item of the day; it had come off the wall and was sitting on the worktop. After some tea and home made cake I made a start on the cupboard. I forgot to check if Anna had removed everything from the cupboard, I tilted it towards me so I could get my hands under the back and heard a noise inside the cupboard, followed by a cold feeling running down my legs.
"What's that smell of vinegar Tim?"
Anna called out from the living room.
"Sorry Anna I forgot to check if you had emptied the cupboard."
"Don't worry Tim it's just my home made pickled onions."
Anna appeared at the door as I put the cupboard back on the worktop and stood looking at my now wet smelly trousers.
"Oh Tim you are funny, take them off and I will wash them in the sink then dry them for you. There is a pair of my dear departed Albert's overalls hanging on the back of the larder door."

As I finished putting the cupboard on the wall Anna came in the kitchen with my trousers washed and pressed, as she handed them to me her telephone rang.
“Hello Mrs Short, No; no one gets a mobile signal here, yes he is just putting his trousers back on, I will go and fetch him, Tim it’s your wife.”
“Thank you Anna, hello darling what’s up? I spilt a jar of pickled onions down my trousers and Anna washed them for me. Mrs Tyler is eighty five, what’s up? Ok.”
After the call I smiled at Anna.
“My wife thinks you’re a scarlet woman Anna.”
Anna went red in the face and with a worried look said.
“Your trousers! Tim I never gave it a thought, I am sorry, are you in trouble?”
“The wife wants me to pick up her mother from the railway station, as for the incident of the trousers, don’t give it another thought.”
Anna offered me twenty pounds; I gave her a peck on the cheek and said.
“The cake was lovely put your money away.” Then I left.

Joan the mother in law was waiting outside the railway station looking annoyed and red in the face, she said.
"Where have you been? I have been waiting ages."
"Trying to earn some money, what do you think I've been doing? Perhaps next time try catching a bus instead of using me as a taxi service."
She never said another word all the way home then went indoors without speaking, that was a bonus in its self.

I drove off to my next job but within five minutes of dropping Joan off my mobile phone rang; Pulling over to the kerb I reluctantly answered It was Sally, she sounded like a mad woman and calling me all the names under the sun, then told me she was taking Susan to stay at her mothers for the weekend, I thought I just can't win. What have I done to deserve all this bad luck?

My next job was at a care home, a ramp had become dislodged and needed securing to the step at the rear door; this seemed a simple job, nothing could go

wrong this time surely! I removed the ramp to drill some new holes; After drilling the holes I slid the ramp back and went to the van for some raw plugs, as I reached the van I heard the back door open, I Rushed back just in time to see a wheel chair appear in the doorway. Unable to reach the ramp in time I watched as the ramp slid down off the steps sending the occupant and wheelchair speeding down the car park. Running as fast as my legs could carry me I followed, my heart was in my mouth as I saw it crash through the bushes followed by a thud, as I cleared the bushes I heard singing, there up against the compost heap was the wheel chair and the occupant singing.
"Roll out the Barrel."
The man was well and truly intoxicated and clutching a bottle of whisky, both the man and wheel chair looked fine although a bit smelly, he was still singing as I pushed him back up the car park but as he hit a high note he shot his arms straight up in the air sending Whisky all over both of us. After telling a little white lie that I found him

down the garden, I handed him over to one of the staff then finished the ramp.

Feeling good that I had finally earned some money I drove off to my next job. I was about half a mile from my next job when I stopped at a red light. Who pulled up beside me? Yes you've guessed it, a police motorcyclist, as my window was down I stunk of whisky, he pulled me over and got his breathalyser out. Yes, it came up negative but as my explanation made me sound as if I was taking the rise out of him, I had to follow him back to his station for a blood test. No one at the station believed me until I got them to phone the home and when the home confirmed my story they couldn't stop laughing at me.

I left and got to my next job, this was a new Customer a Mr Gary Peters. Apparently his washing machine had decided to take a walk across the kitchen floor pulling the pipe work off the wall. Lucky for him he had a stopcock in the cellar. Mr Peters seemed a cheerful pleasant man and a good host providing tea and cheese sandwiches. I had just finished and went down to the cellar to turn the main stopcock back on when I heard a loud thud above. I rushed upstairs and into the kitchen to find Mr Peter's unconscious on the kitchen floor; He seemed to have had a heart attack as he was still breathing, I telephoned for an ambulance and then kept an eye on him until he was taken to hospital.

The next door neighbour came round and took my name and phone number but said not to hold my breath about being paid. Apparently this was Mr Peter's second heart attack and doctors had told him another attack could be fatal.

Money seemed to be eluding me so I went back home and sat down with a cup of tea. Feeling a bit depressed I snuggled down on the settee for a doze, just as I started to drift off the telephone rang again, reluctantly I got up and answered it.
"Hello Mr. Short I am Mrs Gale, I wondered if you could do an erection in my back garden."
"Excuse me! What do you mean?"
I replied.

"I have bought a garden shed and would like it erected as soon as possible."
I took the lady's particulars and set off hoping to earn some money at last.

I arrived at Mrs Gale's house which was an end of terrace, this was good as it meant less distance to lug things to the back garden. Mrs Gale looked about fifty years in age and a very tidy woman, well groomed and smelt of Lavender.
Everything was already at hand in the garden so things looked good. I got things ready and started to lay the slabs. After about fifteen minutes she came out with a tray of tea and biscuits.
"Thank you very much Mrs Gale, I could just do with a cuppa but would it be ok if I came into the kitchen for a bucket of water first?"
"Help yourself as I've got to go to the bank."

As I entered the kitchen I could not believe my eyes, the place was filthy and what the original colour of the cooker and worktop was escaped me. I filled the bucket then went out and emptied the cup of tea down the drain and the biscuits went over the fence to the next doors dog.

Mrs Gale returned later, I had all but finished with just the shed door to hang.
"Hello Mr Short I'm back, would you like a top up?"
"That's very kind but I am just off to have my dinner."
I finished up and she paid me.
As I went out the back gate the next door's dog was in the ally sitting in front of me wagging his tail, I told him no more biscuits and called him a good boy but as I started walking away he shot forward and bit me in the back of the calf.

As he drew blood I ended up at casualty to have a tetanus injection. After sitting in the waiting area for about an hour and twenty minute's I was called. I entered the consulting room and rolled up my sleeve, the bad luck continued as a young nurse told me to drop my trousers and bend over. After the jab she put a solution of peroxide on the wound. "Ouch" talk about rubbing salt in the wound. I left the hospital with my pride in taters, a plaster on my throbbing leg and a sore backside.

By now the time was 6pm and as Sally and Susan were staying at her mothers for the weekend I bought some chips to take home. I thought I would put a couple of fried eggs on top and then watch a DVD. As we had run out of oil I ended up with what I could only describe as a burnt shredded omelette on my chips still I was starving by now.

About three quarters of the way through the film I was plunged into darkness, after falling over the coffee table I managed to find the torch at the side of the television, I headed for the fuse box in the garage. As the RCD would not stay on I flicked all the mini trip fuses off and put the RCD back. I put the trips on one at a time to locate the circuit that was responsible. The offending trip was the security light and downstairs lights.

Returning to the house I looked outside and the security light at the back was hanging off the wall, probably happened when the gutter fell down. On the ground under the light was a squirrel, I guess it must have bitten the cable and been electrocuted, I thought I would put it down the bottom of the garden then bury it in the morning, feeling sad about the squirrel I picked it up by its tail as I neared the bottom of the garden it suddenly came back to life and in a flash swung up and bit my hand; I stood there with the beam of the torch revealing the squirrel disappearing over the fence when I was startled by a loud crash near the house. Yes, the security light had plunged to the ground and smashed, the only good thing was I could put the lights back on in the house.

After soaking my hand in a bowl of hot water and disinfectant to clean the wound the squirrel had inflicted I watched the end of the DVD, I retired to my bed and I slept like a log.

Apart from my sore leg, hand and backside I felt pleased it was the start of another day, I really hoped I had left all that bad luck behind me from yesterday.

After breakfast I kept looking at the phone hoping it was going to ring and I could start earning money to pay some bills. By 10.45am I had given up hope, I decided to go and wash the van.

As I was washing the van I noticed a crowd of people further down the road, being curious I walked down to have a look. A cat had climbed up its owner's tree in his front garden and couldn't get down. As no one else wanted to risk climbing the tree I thought I would start the day with a good deed, I fetched my ladder and up I went.
I managed to get the cat but as I was almost down the cat decided to leap off me to its owner. The cat leapt about five feet and sunk its claws into its owner's shoulders and its teeth into his owner's nose.
Mr Anderson the cat's owner went berserk insinuating I had thrown the cat at him. Two onlookers in the crowd put him straight but Instead of thanking me he just stormed off into his house. I just can't seem to shake this streak of bad luck.

When I thought about it both days started with me doing a good deed.

I walked back and finished washing my van. As I had earned next to nothing for the last two days I decided to phone some of my old customers, I was hoping they had some work for me.

The first person I tried was Colonel Watson and as luck would have it he needed his stables roof mended as the wind had caught a piece of the felt and torn it back letting the rain in. Finally a job that is straight forward and Colonel Watson was a good payer. Luckily there was a roll and a half of felt in his outhouse and a bag of nails left over from when the roof was first done, I fetched his ladder and leaned it against the facer above the window.
I made a good neat job of repairing the roof but Colonel Watson wanted to get up the ladder for his approval, he told me to get his wife while he checked my work; I went over to the house and rang the doorbell.
As Mrs Watson opened the door there was a loud crash from the stables, we both rushed over to see what had happened.

There stood Colonel Watson looking red in the face and staring at my van; He thought he would remove the ladder himself which resulted in the end of the ladder crashing through my passenger's window, he apologised and gave me a hundred pounds for doing the roof, then told me to go to the garage he uses and would instruct them to send him the bill.

I was stuck in the local garage for the best part of the day while they waited for a new window to arrive; while I was waiting I told the owner of the garage about my run of bad luck.
"You have had a bit of good luck Mr Short as there is no film in that speed camera yet so that must cheer you up a little."
It cheered me up quite a bit and while I was there he paid me to clean some of his cars which he had for sale which earned me about thirty pounds. Although I had earned some money today I still needed more for the bills.

I got away from the garage about 3.30pm which never left much time to get another job. Perhaps just one more phone call then I could just relax and try to unwind on Sunday. Lady Philips seemed a good bet as she was always pleased to see me and said we had the same sense of humour. There was no answer so I left a message and headed home.

I had just pulled up outside home as my mobile phone rang, it was Lady Philips apologising for missing my call, she asked if I could pop round straight away if possible. Great I thought, fit this one in then put my feet up for the rest of the evening. Lady Philips lives in a big country home in its own grounds so it needs a lot of maintenance, she has a regular handy man who only works am.

When I arrived there was a note on the front door, (let your self in Tim) I let myself in and stood in the hall and I called out to Lady Philips.
"Hello Tim I will be right down, go in the study."
Lady Philips was in her mid fifties and always well groomed, she was young for her age and a bit of a laugh and she was always smiling and very down to earth.

She appeared in the doorway with a big smile on her face and wearing a short dress straight out of the thirties.
“What do you think Tim? How do I look?”
“You look dazzling lady Philips, what job have you got for me?”
“I just need company for the evening Tim, I will pay you for your time.”
“Where is Lord Philips, Surly he will keep you company?”
“He has gone to London to his club and won’t be back till tomorrow night.”
“What have I got to do? Only if it’s a thirties evening I can’t dance, especially the Charleston but I can watch you.”
She took my hand, pulled me towards her and started to dance the smooch with me. Feeling very awkward, I humoured her but started feeling aroused.
“I think I had better go before I forget myself Lady Philips.”
She walked over to her writing desk, opened a drawer and took out an envelope and smiled as she put it in my inside pocket.
“You will change your mind when you open it, come on enjoy yourself.”

I felt a bit panicky and trembled from head to toe; she was very desirable but I was still very much in love with my wife Sally. I could never look Sally in the face again if I went astray. Lady Philips poured herself a big glass of gin and tonic and asked what I would like to drink.
"I will have to give the drink a miss only I don't fancy using a push barrow instead of my van."
"Sit down and take your jacket off, Just relax and have a laugh." She remarked.
Just telling jokes and talking I could live with which was harmless, I watched her dance the Charleston and listened to her jokes.
By the time she refilled her glass our sides ached from laughing at her jokes and sense of humour, as she finished half a bottle of Gin she sat next to me and snuggled her head into my neck putting her arm across my chest. I started to panic and wished I had left earlier so I made an excuse that I needed to use the toilet, she never budged or answered she was drunk and fast asleep, I carefully shifted her round and laid her on the settee then covered her up with the

throw off the back of the settee. That was the first bit of luck I had had and the second was when I was about half of a mile from the property I passed Lord Philips driving home, he must have changed his mind about the club.

I arrived home, made a cheese and onion sandwich and a cup of tea. It was 9.40pm just enough time to watch a DVD. As the film started I remembered the envelope Lady Philip's had put in my jacket pocket, I took it out and feeling exited I opened it and found twenty pounds inside and a note saying (The other eighty pounds is in my bedroom, give you it after?"
It was worth losing the eighty pounds not to let Sally down. I felt relieved nothing happened and at least I could sleep easy that our marriage was still very special, apart from the mother in-law.
After the film I went to bed looking forward to a relaxing stress free Sunday and was so exhausted I slept soundly.

The telephone woke me about nine am but I was determined not to get involved in any jobs today so I turned over and let it ring. The answer machine clicked in but I couldn't hear the message.

Feeling hungry and thirsty I finally rolled out of bed about 9.45am and had my breakfast before having a shower and getting dressed. What a wonderful feeling the whole day to myself, the trouble was all I could think of doing was mending the greenhouse and the security light, Why? Because that was all my life had consisted of mending things, apart from watching the odd DVD I had no social life.

Determined to do something different I drove to the local keep fit centre, they took in none members for ten pounds a day. First thing I tried was the rowing machine but all that did was make my head spin. The exercise cycle was next which seemed ok until my foot slipped off the pedal and nearly took the skin off my ankle, although my ankle was painful I decided to try the treadmill. I felt great as I quickened up the pace and I felt like I was as light as air, till I missed my footing and fell flat on my face. The next thing I remember was a crowd of people looking down at me and

one of the instructors asking if I was hurt. "No just my big feet getting carried away, just had the wind knocked out of me."
After the instructor checked me over and gave me a cup of coffee he suggested I go home and rest, he took particulars and I left giving it up as a bad idea.
Twenty past eleven and so far the day was a flop. By now I was really missing my wife and daughter so I decided to go home and ask when they would be coming home.

I arrived home and headed straight for the phone, before I phoned I thought I would see who had left a message earlier. "Hello Tim its Sally, can you pick us all up from my mums as she is paying for us to go to France for the day? So if you can get us to the airport in time to catch the 12.15pm flight I will make it up to you, 'love you'."
I phoned straight back but got no reply, it was 11.55am I thought they must have got a taxi so I headed for the airport.

I arrived at the airport and headed straight to the information desk and asked where the 12.15pm flight was, the lady pointed out the window at a plane which had just taken off; I felt really bad about letting them down, what could I do to make it up to them? I stood there watching the plane soar into the sky when it was blotted from view by black smoke engulfing it; I ran outside and as I did the noise of its engines stopped! The plane silently emerged from the black cloud of smoke and plummeted to the ground sending a ball of flame high into the sky as it hit the ground about a mile away.

For a while I just stared at the smoke in the distance having no feeling in my body except a giddy tingling in my head. I rushed to the departure desk and asked if Mrs Short, her daughter and mother had left on the twelve fifteen flight to France.

"Are you Mr Short?"

"Yes I am."

"Yes they did and you're in the doghouse, they nearly missed their flight because of you, your wife was furious."

The lady was not aware the plane had crashed, it started to sink in and the tears started streaming down my face, as I turned to walk back to my van I felt completely empty inside with nothing to look forward to except an empty house, it was full of my wife's and daughter's belongings and the memories that went with them. My life seemed so empty without them and I had to admit it I was even going to miss the mother in-law, even though her ambition was to make my life hell. Most people would have got drunk and smoked as many cigarettes as they could but as I had given up both there was nothing to numb my grief.

How I got home in the van I cannot remember as the tears kept streaming down my face. I stood looking at our house from the van with a feeling of dread coming over me at going into the house. As I reached the front door I turned away and headed back to the van hoping it was all a bad dream, perhaps I would wake up and everything was back to normal, I felt I wanted to die so I could be with Sally and Susan again but I was still in denial hoping for a miracle. As the plane exploded on impact who was I fooling?

I drove to the top of the multi story car park and walked over the edge and then looked over. As my eyes tried to focus on the ground I felt giddy and slumped back and after sitting for awhile I decided to drive to the river, why? I was not thinking straight but under the circumstances seemed to be the right thing to do.

I walked alone the river path and was passing a barge tied up to its moorings, as I came level with the barge a dog on the barge started barking and a man appeared on deck.
“Ignore him it’s the high light of his day, he thinks the river belongs to him.”
As his words rang out the dog got so carried away he fell over board, I rushed to the edge and looked down at the dog whimpering and struggling to stay afloat, I looked at the man.
“I can’t swim.” He cried in panic.
Without thinking I jumped in grabbed the dog then hung on to the tie rope waiting for the man to pull us up but before the man could respond two joggers had

jumped over to the barge and pulled us both out of the water.
“We saw it all, well done mate.”
The joggers said as they patted me on my soggy back then jumped off the barge and carried on with their jog.
The man hugged his dog thanked me and suggested I went below and dried off.
As I didn’t want to go home yet I agreed.
The man introduced himself as Mr Fred Stone and the dog as Teddy a small Yorkshire terrier. Mr Stone was so grateful he said he only used the barge on Sundays so any other day I was welcome to use the barge to treat my family, he handed me a piece of paper with his address and phone number on it. I couldn’t bring myself to tell him what had happened. By the time I had dried off it was four thirty and after saying goodbye I headed back to my van and decided go home.

I pulled into my drive and noticed Lord Philips car parked in the road, I put my key in the lock and heard footsteps behind me, I turned to see Lord Philips striding up the path.

“Mr Short I want a word with you, my wife told me everything.”
As he got within four feet of me he started to reach into the inside of his jacket, I noticed something was bulging under the jacket, he is going to shoot me I thought and froze but as he pulled his hand out I saw he had his wallet in his hand.
“My wife and I are really grateful to you for responding when she locked herself out, If I hadn’t changed my mind about my club she would have been in trouble without your help especially in her drunken state.”
“My pleasure, you are very nice people and have always been fair with me.”
He shook my hand and said.
“You forgot to take this, my wife wants you to have eighty pounds and here is fifty from me.”
Putting the money in my hand he smiled and walked back to his car.

I let myself in and sat on the settee thinking how nice Lady Phillips was but the money didn’t seem that important anymore, I had only sat there feeling lost for a few minutes when the doorbell rang.

I felt near to tears as I new it would be the police to give me the bad news.
I reluctantly opened the front door.
Instead of the police it was Mr Anderson whose cat had been stuck up his tree, well if he wants a fight he can have it I thought.
"Mr Short I want to apologise about earlier and as a way of an apology and a thank you I would like you to take your family for a week's free holiday in our caravan at St Ives."
He put his hand out and shook my hand.
"Just let me know when you want it."
I watched him until he disappeared up the road then I went back to the settee.

My head was in a spin and I was unable to think straight, if only Sally and Susan were here they would have loved a holiday at St Ives and trips on the barge.
I got up to make a cup of tea and noticed I had another message.
"Hello Mr Short its Gary Peters, I just called to thank you for getting the ambulance, apparently I died in the ambulance but the crew got me back, yes you saved my life so if you can pop round sometime I would like

to thank you in person and pay for the work you done on the washing machine."
I stood there thinking that I had done good deeds for people and have been repaid by having my family taken from me, how unfair is that? I made some tea and sat looking at the photo of us all and wondered how I was going to cope without them.

An hour went by then came a loud banging on the front door, what now I thought, it must be the police finally. I had only just started to open the front door when a voice shouted.
"What do you think you're playing at, you just couldn't be bothered to take us to the airport could you?"
The door was pushed open and there stood a red faced Sally and tired looking Susan. I grabbed them and hugged them tightly as tears ran down my face.
"I love you both so much, I thought you were dead."
"Get off you mental case, what are you talking about? What gave you that idea?"
"I never got your message till it was too late so I went to the airport to see you off,

your flight crashed seconds after take off."
"Our plane was faulty, a pilot was taking it to be repaired when it crashed and he bailed out, he is ok so no one was hurt, they gave us another plane in its place."

I explained everything that had happened and stuck to Lady Philips version about her being locked out making Sally laugh and Susan called me silly. I was over the moon and we all cuddled up on the settee for the evening and watched a DVD before going to bed.

The next day, Monday morning we dropped off Susan at her school and Sally and I went to see Mr Peters, he was very happy to see us and invited us to have dinner with him, we did not have to pick Susan up from school till three pm so we accepted.

Mr Peters was the chairman of a chain of factories, he offered me a steady job as a supervisor in charge of maintenance, I declined because I was going to look for an eight till five job as I wanted to spend more time with my

family.
After dinner Mr Peters suggested a job as his manager and said I could fix my own hours; he needed to take more time off due to his heart problem, I excepted even though I felt I was still in a weird dream.

Life was wonderful and we became a very happy family spending all the time we could together. We had our week at St Ives and spent a lot of time on the barge and became very good friends with Fred and Teddy.

I hope you make time to spend with your family because your luck may not turn around like mine; good luck.

You never know how lucky you are or appreciate what you have until you lose it

All the very best

Tim Short

Printed in Great Britain
by Amazon